SNARF ATTACK, UNDERFOODLE, AND THE SECRET OF LIFE

SNARF ATTACK, UNDERFOODLE, AND THE SECRET OF LIFE

The Riot Brothers Tell All

by MARY AMATO

illustrated by

ETHAN LONG

SCHOLASTIC INC.

New York Toronto London Auckland Sydney
Mexico City New Delhi Hong Kong Buenos Aires

ISBN 0-439-69897-9

Text copyright © 2004 by Mary Amato. Illustrations copyright © 2004 by Ethan Long. All rights reserved. Published by Scholastic Inc., 557 Broadway, New York, NY 10012, by arrangement with Holiday House, Inc. SCHOLASTIC and associated logos are trademarks and/or registered trademarks of Scholastic Inc.

12 11 10 9 8 7 6 5 4 3 2 1   4 5 6 7 8 9/0

Printed in the U.S.A.   40

First Scholastic printing, September 2004

For my sons,
Simon and Max,
and in memory of my father, Jack Koepke,
who always had a twinkle in his eye
M. A.

For Tim,
my brother at heart
E. L.

CONTENTS

Book Three
THE RIOT BROTHERS OVERTHROW A KING

BOOK ONE

THE RIOT BROTHERS CAPTURE A CROOK

ONE
Eat Your Green Beans

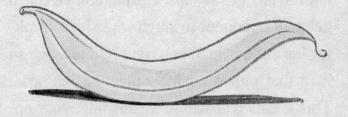

I, Wilbur Riot, was playing Snarf Attack when I discovered the Secret of Life.

What is the Secret of Life, you ask?

Good question. I'll tell you in a minute.

But first, let me tell you about Snarf Attack. This is just one of the many games I've invented. I am very good at inventing games. Some day I plan to write a book about all my games. When I do, you should buy it because then you'll be able to play them, and I'll make a lot of money.

I especially like inventing games for the dinner table because it is boring to sit and do nothing but eat. Snarf Attack is a perfect dinner table game. Here's how you play. Before dinner starts, agree to play Snarf Attack with an opponent, such as your brother. Do not tell any grown-ups. During dinner, try to get your opponent to laugh while he is drinking his milk. In fact, you want him to laugh so hard that milk actually comes out his nose. This is called snarfing. Meanwhile, your opponent will be trying to make you snarf, so keep your eyes open, your mouth shut, and your nostrils on alert.

Just last night, my brother Orville and I were playing Snarf Attack. During the first few minutes, we didn't look at each other. We didn't touch our milk. We just ate our macaroni and stared at our mom like she was the most interesting thing in the world.

But I had a plan. Out of the corner of my eye, I was watching to see when Orville would drop his guard.

"There's chocolate cake for dessert to-night," Mom announced.

"Sweet!" Orville said, and reached for his milk. "Can I have two pieces?"

This was my chance. I pretended to blow my nose, but really I stuck a green bean in my right nostril. "Orville," I said in an ordinary voice. "Please pass the salt."

Orville took a big gulp of his milk and passed me the salt shaker.

I grinned like a mutant Mr. Potato Head. Orville saw that green bean hanging off my face, and he gurgled. A little milk dribbled down his chin, but he didn't laugh. Before Mom could see, I closed my left nostril and blew. The bean flew out and landed on Orville's plate. That did it. He laughed, and milk sprayed out his nose.

SCORE!

"Orville Riot, that was disgusting," Mom said.

"Truly disgusting," I agreed. "You should be ashamed of yourself, Orville. Now, eat your green beans. They're good for you."

My mom looked at me suspiciously. "Since when are you a fan of vegetables?"

I held up a bean and smiled. "Green beans are my friends."

Orville snorted and kicked me under the table. He was giving me his famous I'm-Going-To-Get-You look. For a third grader, he is very good at making faces. He reminded me of the way the third little pig must have looked when he was putting the kettle full of boiling water under the chimney for the wolf. He was determined to make me snarf all over the table.

I needed a plan. I looked at my milk with despair. A full glass to go! Then, a brilliant idea came to me. If I thought of something sad and drank all my milk in one gulp, I wouldn't have anything to snarf. It would be over.

What was sad? I stared at my plate. I imagined what it would be like to be a poor little string bean. What a miserable life. To lie on a plate in a puddle of butter. Only to end up chomped between giant teeth. O cruel fate! How could it get any worse?

Quickly I started to swallow my milk, which was hard because every muscle in my body was tense. Why was Orville staring at me? This was his opportunity. Why wasn't he cracking a joke?

I kept swallowing. I was almost done! One more gulp, and I could see the bottom of my—

A hairy black spider was in the bottom of my glass! *"BLECH!"* I screamed, spraying milk all over my macaroni.

"Got you!" Orville laughed and tipped the plastic spider out of my cup.

"Doesn't count as a snarf! The milk came out my mouth, not my nose."

Mom shook her head, looking almost as miserable as a green bean. "Why can't we have a nice, ordinary dinner?"

I looked at Orville. Orville looked at me.

"Who wants to have a nice, ordinary dinner?" I asked, wiping my mouth on my

T-shirt. "We want suspense. We want excitement. Right, Orville?"

"Bingo bongo, Wilbur. And there's one more thing."

"What's that?"

"We want dessert."

That made Mom laugh. She and Orville started clearing the table, but I was deep in thought. The green beans on my plate were trying to tell me something.

"Orville," I whispered, pulling him back into the dining room. "I think I've discovered the Secret of Life."

His big brown eyes got bigger. "What is it?"

I held up a green bean. "If you wait around like a green bean for something to happen, you'll be bored." I tossed the bean back on my plate.

"That's the Secret of Life?"

"No. The Secret of Life is NOT to be a green bean. The Secret of Life is NOT to wait around. The Secret of Life is to *make* adventure."

"How?"

"How did we make dinner interesting?"

"We played Snarf Attack."

"Right! How do you make life interesting? You need a mission. You have to decide to do something and then do it. We'll make it a rule. Riot Brother Rule Number One: Make something exciting happen every day. We'll start tomorrow."

"What'll we do? Stick *two* green beans up our noses?"

"No."

"How about carrots?"

"No, Orville. We need a thrilling, adventurous mission." An idea popped into my brain. "I've got it. We'll capture a criminal!"

TWO
Got Any Money?

"Wilbur, wake up." Orville poked me. "What kind of crook are we going to catch?"

I opened my eyes. It was morning. There was no time to waste. "Good question, Orville. A jewel thief or a bank robber?"

"A bank robber!" Orville said. "Where do we find one?"

Good thing one of us has the brains. "We find a bank robber at a bank, of course."

"How do we get to the bank?"

"We ask Mom to drive us," I said as I hopped into my clothes.

"When she asks us why we want to go to the bank, what do we say?"

"Why does anybody want to go to the bank? To put money in or take money out."

"But Wilbur, we don't have any money to put in or take out."

He was right! I was stumped. Then the solution came to me. "First, we earn some money. Then, we tell Mom we want to put it in the bank."

Mom walked in holding a cup of tea. The steam from her tea was fogging up her glasses. "What are you two plotting?"

"We're going to earn some money," Orville said. "And then we want to put it in the bank."

I elbowed him so he wouldn't say any more and whispered: "Riot Brother Rule Number Two: Do not tell anyone your true mission."

After breakfast, we made a list of ways to earn money. We had to work quickly because it was a school day, and it was almost time to go to school. This was our list:

IDEAS
1. Sell lemonade.
2. Wash cars.
3. Shovel snow.
4. Have a garage sale.
5. Give piano lessons.

The only problem was that each of the ideas had a problem. So, we had to make a list of the problems.

PROBLEMS

1. **Lemonade Problem:**
   Who wants to buy lemonade
   in January?

2. **Car Wash Problem:**
   The soap and water would probably
   freeze on the cars.

3. **Snow Shoveling Problem:**
   No snow.

4. **Garage Sale Problem:**
   No garage.

5. **Piano Lesson Problem:**
   No piano . . . and we don't know
   how to play.

"What are we going to do?" Orville shrieked.

"We have to think of something that we are really good at doing," I said.

Orville picked his nose. "Mom says we're really, really good at being annoying."

I crumpled up our lists and threw them in the air. "We'll give annoying lessons!"

THREE
Flying Quarters

Orville and I met in the southeast corner of the playground during the first minute of recess. The blacktop was icy. The air was frosty. Within nanoseconds, a crowd of third, fourth, and fifth graders gathered around us.

Why, you ask?

Because we put up these brilliant signs all over the school:

Take Annoying Lessons
from the Famous
Riot Brothers
When: During Recess Today!
Where: The Playground
Cost: The first lesson is free!
After that, only 25¢ per lesson

I clapped my mittens together to get everyone's attention. "Ladies and gentle-men, step right up to get your Annoying Lessons!" I began. "As we promised, the first lesson is free. And here it is. . . ."

I hadn't actually planned what we'd teach. Now, I couldn't think of one single annoying thing.

I turned to my brother. "Orville, you can teach the first lesson."

For a third grader, Orville is pretty good at fast thinking. But the crowd was making him nervous. He wouldn't even look me in the eye. He just stared at my chin as if it were suddenly the most interesting body part in the world. How incredibly annoying.

Did I just say that Orville was being annoying?

I smiled at the audience. "Lesson Number One is being demonstrated right now by my brother Orville."

Orville's eyes practically popped out of their sockets.

I continued. "When someone is talking to you, stare at the person's chin like this." I stared at Margaret Lew's chin. It had spaghetti sauce on it.

"Stop it!" she yelled, and pulled her hat over her face.

"See? It drives people crazy."

There was silence on the playground, and then the crowd burst into mitten-muffled applause.

"Now, if you want to hear Lesson Number Two, give us twenty-five cents." I pulled off Orville's hat and held it out. Quarters, dimes, and nickels flew into it. It was working! It may have been freezing cold on that playground, but baby, we were hot.

"Can you think of another lesson to teach?" Orville whispered.

"I can think of a million. We're going to be rich!" I whispered back. Then I turned to the crowd. "Lesson Number Two goes like this. Whenever a grown-up asks you a question, you start singing 'la, la, la.'"

More silence. I couldn't tell if they liked it or not.

"Orville and I will now demonstrate," I said. "Pretend I am a teacher." I lowered my voice. "Orville Riot, what is the capital of Nebraska?"

Orville grinned and crossed his eyes and stuck out his tongue. "La, la, la, la, la!"

The crowd cheered.

"You can do this anywhere, anytime!" I said.

"Especially in Mr. Martin's class!" Orville added. The crowd cheered louder. Mr. Martin is our music teacher. His room smells like something furry died in it.

I held out Orville's hat. "Pay up for Lesson Number Three!"

The quarters, dimes, and nickels practically had wings on them.

"Lesson Number Three goes like this. If someone tells you to do something you don't want to do, just keep asking questions."

"What do you mean?" a kid asked.

Before I could answer, Goliath Hyke
stomped up. Goliath is a fifth grader who
wears a strange pointy hat that makes him
look like a rogue warrior from another
planet. He missed the first part of our lecture
because he had detention for pouring milk on
Jonathan Kemp's spaghetti.

Why did Goliath Hyke pour milk on
Jonathan Kemp's spaghetti, you ask?

Goliath Hyke doesn't need a reason.

Now, Goliath was glaring at me. He probably didn't like the way everybody was gathered around me. He probably wanted to pour milk on me. "Break it up," he said.

"Here's your chance to demonstrate Lesson Number Three," Orville whispered.

The crowd was silent.

Goliath took a giant step toward me. "I said break it up."

"Break what up?" I asked innocently.

"Break up this crowd, dough-head."

"You mean these students? How can we break up students? Wouldn't that be harmful to their health?"

"Don't get smart with me!" He was getting mad. I didn't know if annoying him further was such a good idea.

Then Orville chimed in. "If the purpose of school is to get smart, then how can you tell us not to get smart?"

Goliath looked down at Orville as if he were a pesky bug. For a third grader, Orville is very short. "Get lost," Goliath said.

Orville looked up. I was sure Goliath was about to crush him beneath his boot. But bless my brother's buggy heart, he didn't panic. Orville fired off more questions. "How can I get lost if I know where I am? Or, what if I get lost and someone finds me? Then will I be found even if I'm still lost?"

Goliath growled, his breath puffing like smoke in the cold air. "You guys are really annoying."

"Ladies and Gentlemen, you heard it here!" I exclaimed. "We are experts at annoying, and now you're learning all our tricks." I held out Orville's hat. "Pay up for Lesson Number Four. Only twenty-five cents."

My brother smiled sweetly. "Don't you want to learn it, Goliath? It's the best one yet."

Goliath growled again, but to our amazement, he pitched in a quarter, saying: "This better be good."

BLAST OFF went the other kids' quarters, dimes, and nickels. Just as the coins crash-landed in Orville's hat, the bell rang.

"Sounds like recess is over," I said, and started jogging toward the door, the coins jingling merrily in the hat. Orville followed.

"What about Lesson Number Four?" somebody called.

With my free hand, I waved back at the crowd. "Lesson Number Four: Collect money for a lesson, and then run out of time before you can teach it."

FOUR
Coffee, Anyone?

We made $19.50. Plenty of money to open up a bank account and catch a crook.

After recess we stuffed all the coins into our pockets.

"Those signs really did the trick!" I said. "We're brilliant!"

"We're rich!"

"We're jingly!"

"We're fat!" Orville danced around, jingling.

"I'd love to stay and jingle with you," I said. "But it's time to go to class."

Orville danced off to language arts. I had music.

It's very hard to concentrate on school when you're about to catch a bank robber. I kept imagining the scene at the bank. We'd probably get a reward for the capture. What would it be? A medal? A trophy? A mountain of money?

"All right, class," Mr. Martin said as he passed out the *Sweet Songs of Youth* books. "Turn to page fourteen. We're going to learn a sad but beautiful song about a dying daffodil. I'll sing a line. You repeat it."

Mr. Martin took a deep breath and sang: "Oh, the poor little daffodil wilting in the rain . . ."

The entire class took a deep breath and sang: "La, la, la, la, la, la, la!"

Except me.

I took a deep breath and sang, "Oh, the poor little daffodil wilting in the rain . . ."

Everybody howled with laughter.

Except Mr. Martin.

"Go explain this to the principal," he said to me.

"Why me?" I asked. "I didn't do anything."

He held up a piece of paper. It looked unfortunately familiar.

Take Annoying Lessons
from the Famous
Riot Brothers
When: During Recess Today!
Where: The Playground
Cost: The first lesson is free!
After that, only 25¢ per lesson

When I got to the principal's office, Orville was already there. I took the seat next to him directly across from the principal's desk.

The principal wasn't looking at us. She was looking at one of our stupid signs and shaking her head. Then she looked at us.

"Wilbur and Orville," she said, still shaking her head.

The principal DOES NOT know the name of every single kid in our school. But I'm embarrassed to admit that she DOES know our names. That's because we've been in her office before.

It's also because she's our mom. Lydia

Riot is the name. Everyone calls her Ms. Riot. Except us, of course. We call her Mom.

"I want to hear what happened in each of your classes," she said.

I told the "la, la, la" story. Mom's eyes rolled. She did not laugh.

Then it was Orville's turn. "Well, Mrs. Pensky was giving us a spelling test," Orville began. "After the first three words, she leaned over to Margaret Lew and whispered: 'Do I have something on my chin?' Margaret didn't answer. She just looked at Mrs. Pensky's chin. So, Mrs. Pensky gave the next four words. And then she got a handkerchief and wiped off her chin. After the next two words, she dug a mirror out of her purse and looked at herself. We only had one more word to go. But before Mrs. Pensky gave it to us, she shouted: 'Why is everybody looking at my chin?' Nobody answered. Everybody just looked at her chin. So, she sent me here."

Mom's eyes rolled again. "And you two actually made money teaching these pranks to your fellow students?"

"Nineteen dollars and fifty cents," Orville said.

Mom whistled. For a principal, she is a good whistler.

"We want to put it in the bank," I added.

"That's a good place to put money, but you're not going to put this money there."

My heart started to sink. We weren't going to catch a crook after all.

Mom held out a coffee can.

"No thanks," said Orville. Perhaps he thought Mom was offering him coffee.

For the third time, Mom's eyes took a spin. (She really should go to an eye doctor about that.) "Boys, put all the money you earned in the can. You're returning it."

We had to empty our brilliant, rich, jingly, fat pockets.

I've got to tell you that the sound of your coins dropping into somebody else's coffee can is the saddest thing in the whole world. Much sadder than a rainy old wilting daffodil.

FIVE
Who Said Errands Are Boring?

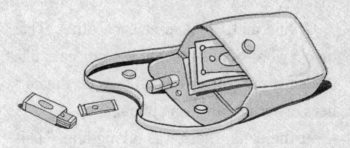

Not only did we have to give back the money, but we also had to stay after school and clean the halls.

When we were done, we went back to the principal's office. Whenever we have to stay after school, the principal gives us a ride home.

"I'm starved," Orville said.

"Well, put your stomach on hold," Mom said as she locked the school doors. "We have to stop somewhere on the way home."

"Not an errand!" Orville complained.

We hate errands.

"I don't want to hear any complaints." Mom unlocked the car doors. "We're stopping at the bank to make a deposit and that's that."

Orville and I looked at each other. That magic word—*bank*—floated to our ears like a wish come true. We tried to keep the corners of our mouths from jumping up.

At the bank, there was a long line. "This will only take two minutes," Mom said.

That was the most ridiculous exaggeration in the universe. Grown-ups say that an errand will take two minutes, and it really takes two centuries. But for once, Orville and I didn't care.

"Where's the robber, Wilbur?" Orville whispered.

As I looked around, it dawned on me that there might not be a bank robber here after all. A bank is certainly a good place for a bank robber to be. But what if the crook was at home right now, deciding to rob the bank tomorrow?

I was about to talk to Orville about this when he grabbed my arm.

"Don't look now! I think I see him."

A chill raced up my spine.

Orville raised one eyebrow and nodded in the direction of a man at the front of the line.

I looked without looking as if I was looking—this is a special Riot Brother skill.

The man had on a long dark coat with the collar turned up. Pulled low over his shifty eyes was a dark hat. On his hands were black gloves. Gloves to keep his fingerprints from getting all over the place.

Nervously, the man kept glancing at the tellers and at the security guard who was asleep in a chair by the door.

Orville was right!

Riot Brother Rule #3
If someone says, "Don't look now!"
make sure you look.

"He's waiting until it's his turn," Orville whispered. "Then he'll go up to the teller and tell her it's a stickup."

We watched breathlessly as the teller on the right gave money to a woman with a furry coat and a nose like a pickle. Pickle Nose put her money in her purse and started to leave.

"Next!" called the teller.

The crook started walking toward the teller. As he walked, he put his right hand in his pocket.

"He's reaching for his weapon!" Orville whispered.

The next part seemed as though it was happening in slow motion. I remember glancing at poor Pickle Nose, wishing that she would walk a little faster so she wouldn't be in the way. I remember thinking: well, at least she's very skinny. If he shoots in her direction, he'll probably miss.

"Do something," Orville hissed.

The man was pulling a small black weapon out of his pocket.

I couldn't just stand there like a green bean. I had to take action. "Stop!" I yelled. "Thief!"

The customers gasped. The tellers screamed. Pickle Nose dropped her purse. The security guard fell out of his chair. And the crook froze with his hands up.

Except he wasn't holding a weapon. He was holding his checkbook. He wasn't a crook.

The bank was completely silent. Although I wasn't looking at my mom, I could tell that she was glaring at me. I didn't know what to do.

Then Pickle Nose picked up her purse, clutched it to her chest, and staggered toward the security guard. Everybody gasped.

"She's having a heart attack," Orville cried. "We scared her to death!"

She opened her purse and pulled out money. She slapped it into the hand of the security guard. "FINE!" she shouted angrily. "I'll confess! The teller gave me five hundred dollar bills instead of five dollar bills."

She turned and glared at me. "How did you know, kid?"

I looked at Orville. He grinned and sang, "La, la!"

SIX
Funderwear

Everybody wanted to shake our hands. Except Pickle Nose.

The bank manager didn't give us a trophy, a medal, or a mountain of money. But the customers in the line let us cut to the front. And the teller gave us lollipops.

"Let's save them," Orville said. "We can spray paint them gold and put them in our Riot Brothers' Trophy Case."

"Not too shabby," I replied. "But we don't have a Riot Brothers' Trophy Case."

Orville ate his.

Two centuries later, we finally made it home. It was six o'clock.

"We have three hours until bedtime," Orville said. "What should we do, Wilbur?"

"I'll tell you what we're going to do," Mom replied, even though her name isn't Wilbur. "We're going to have a *nice* evening. We're going to eat dinner. Then you two are going to wash the dishes nicely and do your homework nicely."

I looked at Orville. Orville looked at me.

"Who wants to have a *nice* evening?" I asked.

"We're not green beans!" Orville said.

"We're the Riot Brothers! We want our evenings to crackle with comedy, drip with danger, and explode with excitement."

Mom gave us a look. "I think we've had enough excitement for one day."

We didn't want Mom to have a heart attack. So, we ate dinner, washed the dishes, and did our homework.

"Bedtime," Mom announced as we closed our books.

"I'm not at all tired," Orville said.

"I'm never tired," I said.

It's true. There is something about bedtime that makes me very awake.

"Let's play Underfoodle!" Orville whispered.

We ran upstairs.

Underfoodle is a game Orville invented when he was in kindergarten. We still play it because for a kindergartner Orville was very good at inventing games. It must run in the family. Here's how you play.

In exactly thirty seconds, you see how many underpants you can get on your head. At the same time, you try to pull underpants off your brother's head. At the end, whoever has the most underwear on his head wins.

"Go!" Orville shouted.

"One, two, three . . ." We pulled out our dresser drawers. Socks and underwear and

arms flew. I put on five before Orville tackled me and pulled two off.

"You fink!" I screamed and yanked off two of his seven.

He scooped up everything in his underwear drawer and jumped on his bed. "It's snowing!" he yelled and threw socks and underwear in the air. Before I could get him, he put three more on.

"Diaper head!" I said.

Orville laughed so hard he snorted.

I tackled him and he screamed.

"What's going on up there?" Mom's voice drifted up the stairs.

"BZZZ!" Orville shouted. "Time's up!"

We looked at the heaps of underwear on our heads and fell on the floor laughing.

"Wait!" I sat up. A saying was coming to me. I like to make up sayings. Someday I plan to write them all down in a book that will inspire millions of people everywhere.

Orville straightened the underwear hat on his head and took a sip of water from the glass by his bed.

I cleared my throat. I said, "All you need is a butt to put underpants on your butt, but it takes a brain to put underpants on your head."

"Good one!" Orville said, with his mouth full of water. And then he snarfed.

The End

BOOK TWO

THE RIOT BROTHERS FIND A HIDDEN TREASURE

ONE
You Never Know

Here's what I, Wilbur Riot, was doing when the surprise came in the mail. I was playing The Naked Mole-Rat Game with my brother, Orville.

I invented this game when Orville and I were at a fancy restaurant where the food didn't even look like food. The only thing we liked were the crackers that come in little packages. So I made up this game.

"Orville," I said. "Let's see if we can eat our crackers in exactly forty-one bites."

"Okay, Wilbur!"

For a third grader, my brother is sometimes actually reasonable.

We nibbled and counted. And the more we nibbled, the more we cracked up. Orville kept looking cross-eyed so he could see his cracker. And when we got to the end, we were practically gnawing on our fingers.

"You look like a naked mole rat!" I said with a mouth full of cracker crumbs.

Orville laughed and blew his crumbs all over the fancy tablecloth.

This is how the Naked Mole-Rat Game was born.

But, Wilbur, what does any of this have to do with the mail, you ask?

Well, Orville and I were playing the Naked Mole-Rat Game at the breakfast table on a cold Saturday in February. We were using toast instead of crackers. Orville had picked the number ninety-nine. We were on bite ninety-seven of ninety-nine and our cheeks hurt from laughing so hard. Then . . . *Thwaap*! A bundle of mail dropped through the slot.

At first, we didn't pay any attention to the mail. We were busy gobbling crumbs off our fingertips. "Ninety-eight, ninety-nine!" I said.

"I won!" Orville yelled.

"No, I won!"

"I won!"

"I won!"

"I won!"

Our mom lowered the newspaper she was reading and stared at us for some reason.

"You both won!" she said, as if that made any sense.

"Go get the mail," I said to Orville. "Maybe there's something good in it for us."

Orville ran to the front door, picked up the mail, and ran back to the table.

"Must you run everywhere?" Mom asked.

"Riot Brother Rule Number Four," I re-
cited. "Run, do not walk, whenever possible."

She rolled her eyes.

Orville whipped through the mail, handing
me each letter after he looked at it.

Here's what was in the mail.

1. No birthday invitations
2. No coupons for free ice cream
3. No gift packages from forgotten
    relatives
4. No postcard from the President of
    the United States
5. No ransom note from a kidnapper
6. No offer to . . .

"Wait!" I said. I felt a saying coming on.
Sayings come to me naturally because, for a
fifth grader, I am very wise.

Orville sat down and listened politely.

I cleared my throat. "Life is like the mail,"
I said. "You can't count on something exciting to come through the slot."

"Good one, Wilbur," Orville said, hopping back up. "What do we do now?"

"Riot Brother Rule Number One: Make something exciting happen every day."

"How about we write ourselves a letter?"

"Not too shabby," I said. "But it wouldn't be a surprise. For something to be truly exciting, it has to be a surprise."

It was hard to think because our mom was being very noisy. She has a habit of talking.

"Here's a letter for old Mr. Hally," she said. "He died over twelve years ago!"

We weren't even going to ask who Mr.

Hally was, but she kept talking. "Mr. Hally was the man who owned the house before us." She laughed. "This place was like a museum when we bought it, stuff piled from floor to ceiling. He was a crazy old squirrel."

As she talked, my brain-gears were spinning. "Orville," I whispered. "What if old Mr. Hally left a treasure hidden somewhere in the house?"

Orville's eyes got huge. "Like bags of candy?"

"Well, I was thinking more about gold or jewels."

"And what if we find it?"

"That's what we're going to do today!" I whispered. "We're going to find a hidden treasure!"

"Bingo bongo!" Orville jumped up. Then he sat down. "But if we know we're going to find a hidden treasure, how can it be a surprise?"

For a moment, Orville had me. Then it came to me: "The surprise is that we don't know where it's hidden."

"Right!" said Orville. "Let's do it!"

Have You Ever Tried Picking Up 1,000 Paper Clips?

"Let's start in the basement!" We jumped up and ran to the basement door.

"Stop!" Mom yelled. "It's family cleanup time."

Our bodies froze on the top step. "NO!" we groaned.

"Wilbur vacuums. Orville dusts. Start in the den. Don't forget to pick up anything off the floor before you vacuum."

"But we have something important to do!" I yelled back.

"Clean up before you do it," she said.

Clean *before?* That didn't make any sense. "You're cruel!" I yelled.

"No, I'm not," she replied. "I'm Mom." She actually laughed.

Orville and I got all the cleaning junk and met in the den. "We have to hurry," I said.

Orville picked a penny off the floor. "See a penny, pick it up. All day long you'll have good luck." He put it in his pocket and looked at the mess. "I wish we were lucky enough to have one machine that could do all the work."

"I've got it!" I said. "Why don't we invent an attachment to the vacuum that picks up stuff off the floor and another attachment that dusts furniture? We'll finish our work three times faster."

"What will we call it?"

"Excellent question!"

We made a list.

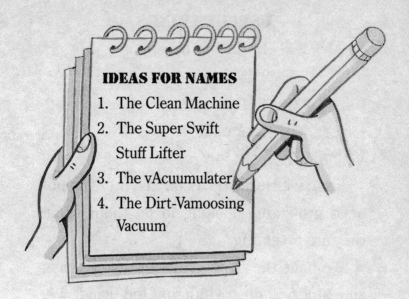

IDEAS FOR NAMES

1. The Clean Machine
2. The Super Swift
   Stuff Lifter
3. The vAcuumulater
4. The Dirt-Vamoosing
   Vacuum

"I vote for Super Swift Stuff Lifter, Wilbur."

"Excellent choice," I said. It happened to be my idea.

We ran around the house collecting useful things.

"Are you cleaning?" Mom asked as we whizzed past her.

"YES!" we said.

Here is what we collected.

USEFUL THINGS

1. Rubber bands
2. Masking tape
3. A hanger
4. A rake

First, we closed the door. Inventors do not need grown-ups looking in on them when they are inventing.

We bent the hanger to look like an arm and stuck a dust cloth on the hand. We attached this to one side of the vacuum with rubber bands. While pushing the vacuum, the arm would swing to the side and dust passing furniture.

Then we attached the rake to the front of the vacuum with masking tape. The rake would push items on the floor to keep them from getting sucked up in the vacuum.

"Turn it on, Orville!" I said when we were ready.

There was a knock on the door. "I haven't

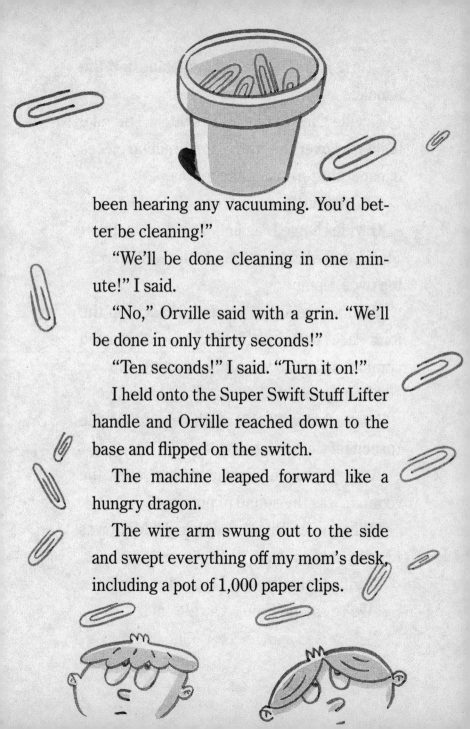

been hearing any vacuuming. You'd better be cleaning!"

"We'll be done cleaning in one minute!" I said.

"No," Orville said with a grin. "We'll
be done in only thirty seconds!"

"Ten seconds!" I said. "Turn it on!"

I held onto the Super Swift Stuff Lifter
handle and Orville reached down to the
base and flipped on the switch.

The machine leaped forward like a
hungry dragon.

The wire arm swung out to the side
and swept everything off my mom's desk,
including a pot of 1,000 paper clips.

"Turn it off!" I yelled, grabbing for the handle.

Orville tried to reach the switch. The rake bulldozed over the trash can. A million pieces of paper fluttered out like moths.

"Turn it off!"

Orville lunged again. The Super Swift Stuff Lifter slammed against the wall, knocking over a lamp.

With a screech, it started to suck up the long lace curtains. Stinky smoke started coming out of the vacuum's mouth.

Mom opened the door.

I wrestled with the machine, and Orville turned off the switch.

A very peaceful sound floated over the room. It was the sound of nothing.

"What on earth are you doing?" Mom was looking at the mess.

Orville looked at me. I looked at Orville.

"We're saving time," Orville said.

THREE
Messy Closets Rule

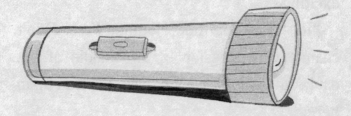

Mom didn't even offer to help clean up. She said she had work of her own and left us alone.

"Sorry," Orville said to the Super Swift Stuff Lifter as we took it apart. "We know you tried."

I threw away a gob of masking tape. "The reason it didn't work is because this room is too messy. We should try it on a completely empty room."

"Bingo bongo! Let's do it!"

"We can't. We have to find the treasure."

"I was thinking," Orville said. "What if there isn't a treasure for us to find? Maybe we should pick a new mission. How about saving someone from doom? That would be exciting."

"Riot Brother Rule Number Five: Don't change your mission in the middle of the day! And besides, we still have to clean up in here."

"Well, I can't do any more cleaning," Orville said. "I ran out of dust cloths."

Mom's voice came from the hallway: "There is a big white bag of clean rags in the closet."

Riot Brother Rule #6:
Talk softly even if you think you're alone,
because grown-ups have excellent hearing.

Orville stuck his head in the closet. "I don't see them."

"Use your hands!" she called out.

Orville stuck his hands in the closet and shook them around. "I still don't see them!"

I got a flashlight and squeezed in with Orville. We stepped on a big white bag with something soft in it, and I flashed the light around.

Hanging up: old coats. On the floor: a box of dead batteries, a large painting, and lots of dust. In the corner: Dracula with blood dripping from his fangs.

Orville screamed and bumped against me. I dropped the flashlight and bumped against the wall. The painting fell over with a crash.

Dracula didn't move one fang. That's because Dracula was made out of plastic.

"It's my old Halloween mask!" I said.

We both started cracking up.

Then I noticed something new. The flashlight was shining on a wooden box covered with dust. It had been hidden behind the painting.

My insides got all jumpy with excitement.

"Well, well, well." I picked it up. "What do we have here?"

Orville shined the flashlight on the box.

It was about the size of a dictionary with vines carved in the top. On the side was a brass lock.

I looked at Orville. Orville looked at me.

"Mr. Hally's hidden treasure!"

"There's only one problem," I said.

"What's that?"

"No key!"

We searched everywhere. No luck.

"Should we ask Mom if she knows where the key is?" Orville asked.

"ARE YOU CRAZY? We have to keep this a secret."

"Should we break it open?"

"ARE YOU CRAZY? The *box* is probably worth money."

"Should we take it to the hardware store and see if they have a key for it?"

"ARE YOU CRAZY? Wait—that's a pretty good idea!"

I wrapped the box in a newspaper and we started to leave the den.

Orville grabbed my arm. "What if the ghost of Mr. Hally wakes up and gets mad at us for stealing his treasure?"

I laughed.

"What's so funny?" Mom asked. She appeared out of nowhere with a mop in her hand.

I concentrated on making my face blank so that she wouldn't suspect anything. I was concentrating so hard that I couldn't think of anything to say. "Uh—what's so funny, Orville?"

Orville let out a great burp.

We laughed.

"You're both very funny," Mom said. "Turn around and get back to work."

FOUR

Shoom . . .
Shoom . . . Yikes!

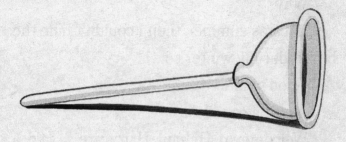

After cleaning up, we asked permission to walk to Helpful Hardware. Helpful Hardware is extremely helpful because it's only three blocks from our house.

"Yes. But only if you pick up a toilet plunger," Mom said, handing us five dollars. "And bundle up. It's freezing."

The walk was treacherous: gusting winds, icy sidewalks. But we marched bravely on, our fingers freezing, our eyes stinging, our noses dripping. Of course, it was much harder for me because I was hugging the treasure box against my chest. No free hand to wipe away the snot.

"We're lucky it's winter," I shouted over the wind to Orville.

"Why?"

"If it was summer, then I couldn't hide the box under my winter coat!"

"Good point."

Finally, we made it.

"Welcome to Helpful Hardware!" said a woman by the door. "May I help you?"

My lips were so cold, I couldn't get them to work. "We're looking for a key," I said. But it came out: "Me mooky a me."

Orville cracked up. His face looked like a tomato about to explode.

"Keys!" I finally said.

She smiled. "Aisle ten!"

We walked down the first aisle and turned the corner.

Orville's grin dropped. "Did you see that?" he whispered.

"See what?"

"Someone is following us."

We turned down an aisle. Orville glanced over his shoulder. "Don't look now!" he whispered.

Of course, I looked. But of course I looked without looking as if I was looking.

An old man came around the corner wearing overalls and a flannel shirt. He had no hair. He had no teeth. His footsteps were slow muffled shuffles: *shoom . . . shoom . . . shoom.*

"It's Mr. Hally's ghost," Orville whispered.

"It is not. It's just an old guy shopping."

"Why isn't he wearing a coat? Ghosts are the only people who don't wear coats in the winter."

I tightened my grip on the box hidden under my coat.

Shoom . . . shoom . . . shoom. He was staring right at us.

"Orville, you may be onto something. Let's keep watching him. But if he stops and picks up anything, then we'll know he's not a ghost."

We pretended to look at door knockers. The old man shuffled right by the toilet plungers and the bird feeders. He wasn't interested in hardware. He was interested in us!

We hurried around the corner into the next aisle.

"What do we do now?" Orville asked.

"Before we panic, we have to find out if he really is a ghost."

"How?"

I had to think fast. "I know! Ghosts don't show up in mirrors. We'll lead him to the mirror aisle and see if we can see his reflection in one."

The old man turned around the corner. *Shoom . . . shoom . . . shoom.*

We passed the mouse traps and kept walking. *Shoom . . . shoom . . . shoom . . .* he followed like a cat on the prowl.

Finally, we saw the mirrors. Halfway down the aisle, I pulled Orville over. We looked into a large mirror in a fancy golden frame. "Just keep looking into this mirror," I said. "When he passes by, we'll see if his reflection passes by!"

Out of the corner of our eyes we saw the old man turn the corner. *Shoom . . . shoom . . . shoom.*

Orville and I held our breath. I gripped the treasure box tightly to my chest.

Closer and closer he came. *Shoom . . . shoom.*

Orville's eyes looked like they were going to pop out and bounce against the mirror like Ping-Pong balls. *Shoom . . . shoom . . . shoom.*

Just a few more steps and he'd pass behind us. *Shoom.*

He stopped.

I looked at Orville in the mirror. Orville looked at me in the mirror. We didn't move.

Why had he stopped before reaching the mirror? There was only one reason. He knew we were giving him a ghost test. And he was a ghost.

He leaned forward and lifted a bony finger. "What's that under your coat?" he hissed.

Orville screamed and knocked into me. We both fell down.

"Shoplifting is against the law!" he said. "What are you trying to hide under your coat?"

Orville and I both noticed the Helpful Hardware name tag on his flannel shirt.

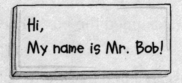

Hi,
My name is Mr. Bob!

"Do ghosts wear name tags?" Orville whispered.

"I don't think so," I replied.

"What was that?" Mr. Bob yelped. "What are you two whispering about? You think you're going to get away with stealing? Not when I'm working! I'm calling the police.

They'll lock you right up. You think you'll *like* being in jail?"

"We're not shoplifters!" I said.

"In fact, we catch crooks," Orville added. "We caught a bank robber just the other day."

It was true. I wrote all about it in *The Riot Brothers Capture a Crook*.

Mr. Bob didn't believe us. "What's that under your coat, then?"

I didn't want to show Mr. Bob the box. But I had to. "We brought this from home. We want to buy a key for it."

Mr. Bob examined the box. "Humph!" he said.

"He's disappointed that we're not going to die in jail," Orville whispered.

"We don't have keys that fit old locks like this," Mr. Bob grumbled. "What do you want a key for anyway?"

Old Bobby wasn't too smart.

"See, it's locked," I explained. I talked

slowly and loudly so he could understand. "To open it, we need a key."

Mr. Bob pinched the sides of the brass lock together and the lock popped open.

Orville and I gasped.

FIVE
Plunging into Doom

Mr. Bob's bony hand began lifting the lid. He was going to see all the gold and jewels gleaming inside! And when he saw them, he'd call the police. The police wouldn't believe our story. They'd put us in jail. We'd be ruined!

"Don't open it!" I shouted.

Mr. Bob almost dropped the box on his bony toes. "Why? What's inside?"

My mind went blank. I looked at Orville. "Tell him what's inside, Orville."

Orville looked up at Mr. Bob. When Orville wants to, he can make his face look like one of those angels painted on a cathedral ceiling. "It's just a dead naked mole rat," he said.

Mr. Bob handed over the box.

I grabbed it, and we flew out the door.

"Let's see what's inside!" Orville said.

"No!" The wind was trying to send us up the Helpful Hardware flagpole. Although I was dying to see what was inside, I knew we had to wait. "What if it's full of hundred dollar bills, and the wind blows them away?"

"Okay, then let's run!"

We took off. It is very hard to run on ice in the wind. Especially when you're holding a hidden treasure.

I was in front of Orville when a truck pulled into a driveway ahead.

I stopped. Orville crashed into me.

Before we both fell, I noticed the sign on the truck: L. H. K. Plumbing.

"We forgot the plungerrrrr!" I said as we plunged.

We had to turn around and run back.

"Now what?" grumbled Mr. Bob.

"We need a plunger."

"We're all out."

"You are not. We saw them."

"Humph," Mr. Bob said, and shuffled away.

We got a plunger and ran to the cashier.

Orville pulled the five dollars out of his pocket.

"$5.01," she said with a smile.

Orville looked at me. I looked at him.

I checked my pockets. Not one quarter. Not one dime. Not one nickel. Not one penny.

"Don't you have a jar with extra pennies?" I asked.

"Sorry!" she said.

"Will you sell it to us for five dollars?"

"Sorry!"

"You aren't being very helpful," I said.

"Open up the box," Orville whispered. "Maybe there's a penny inside."

"No!"

I was just about to give up. Then I remembered something. "It's a good thing we had to clean the den," I exclaimed.

"What?"

"See a penny, pick it up, remember?"

Triumphantly, Orville pulled the lucky penny out of his pocket.

The cashier handed him the plunger and away we ran.

Halfway home, the wind picked up speed. It was at our heels. It was nipping. It was barking.

Wait! It wasn't the wind! It was Doom, our neighbor's huge brown dog with huge brown fangs. He was nipping at MY heels because Orville was in front.

"Help!" I started to slip. I knew that as

soon as I hit the ground, Doom's fangs would be all over my face. My life would be over.

Orville whirled around. With a mighty yell, he leapfrogged over me and thrust the plunger at Doom like a sword. "Back off!" he shouted.

Doom stood still and barked twice.

"Take that!" Orville thrust the plunger at him one more time. Doom sneered, turned around, and trotted home. "Ha!" Orville shouted after him. "Scaredy Dog!"

"Not too shabby," I said.

Orville grinned and raised the plunger high in the air. "We should spray paint this gold—"

"And put it in our Riot Brothers' Trophy Case," I said.

We ran home.

SIX
Who Invented Lips, Anyway?

In the privacy of our bedroom, Orville and I huddled. With a frozen and shaking hand, I opened the lock.

"I get to lift the lid," Orville said.

"I want to," I argued. "I'm the oldest."

"So what?"

"Well, I'm the one who found it in the closet."

"Well, I'm the one Mom told to go in the closet in the first place."

He had something there. "Okay, we'll both open it at the same time."

We each took hold of the lid.

"Gold? Diamonds? Rubies?" I guessed as we lifted it open. Nestled inside were . . .

Two pairs of tiny blue socks. And two tiny blue hats. And two tiny wrist bands:

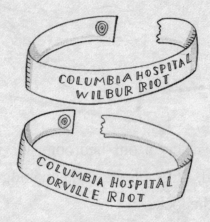

And a bunch of baby photos and papers.

"Baby stuff!" Orville said.

"*Our* baby stuff."

"I can't believe it."

My heart sank like a dead rock.

Mom walked in. "I didn't know you guys were looking through the baby box." She pulled out the photos. "Oh, you were the cutest babies in the world."

"We thought it was a treasure box," I said sadly.

"It is!" She pulled out the papers. "Look at all this stuff."

I was about to fall into a serious depression when something caught my eye.

An important-looking envelope had my name on it. It said: $500.00 Savings Bond. There was another one with Orville's name on it.

"What are these?" I asked.

"Your great grandpa bought those for you when you were born."

"You mean we each have five hundred bucks?"

"Yes, they're bonds. You have to wait until you're eighteen to cash them."

I looked at Orville. Orville looked at me. He grinned. "Not too shabby!"

We opened the envelopes. Inside were the bonds, which looked like money, and a handwritten note.

I pulled out mine. "Give this to Pooky Waddles," I read. "Along with ten thousand smackeroonies from the kissing machine."

Mom laughed. "You don't remember your great grandpa. He called you Pooky Waddles."

"Pooky Waddles!" Orville howled.

I pulled a note out of Orville's envelope and read: "Give Onion-head twenty thousand smackeroonies. He has to catch up."

"Onion-head?" Orville screamed.

It was my turn to laugh.

"What's a smackerooni from the kissing machine?" I asked.

"A smackerooni is a kiss." Mom grinned. "And I'm the kissing machine!" She made kissy lips and came after us.

We screamed and ran.

Halfway down the stairs, I felt a saying coming on. It was hardly the time or place for a saying, but I couldn't help it. "Wait!" I said.

Mom and Orville stopped and listened politely.

I cleared my throat. "There is nothing quite as frightening as your mom chasing after you with kissy lips."

"Good one!" Orville said.

Mom laughed and dove after us, but we were faster. We tore down the stairs, ran into the den, and hid in the closet.

In the darkness, we sat side by side on the floor holding our breath, listening for the sound of the approaching kissing machine, and staring at the closed door in front of our faces.

"Do you feel jingly inside?" Orville whispered.

"What do you mean?"

"When I'm hiding, I get this jingly feeling inside. It's like jingly, jack-in-the-box music.

I want the door to pop open. And I don't want the door to pop open."

"I know what you mean," I whispered. We were quiet for a few seconds.

"Hey Pooky Waddles," he whispered.

"Yes, Onion-head?" I whispered back.

"We found a hidden treasure, didn't we?"

"Yep."

Even though it was too dark to see him, I could hear my brother grin.

"Guess what else?" I whispered.

"What?"

"You saved someone from doom!"

"I did?"

"You saved me from Doom! Get it?"

Orville started to laugh.

Then the kissing machine threw open the door, and we all screamed.

The End

ONE
What's Cookin'?

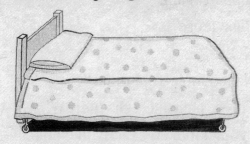

If you're like me, Wilbur Riot, you hate falling asleep. So here is *Riot Brother Rule #7: Stay awake as long as possible.*

One night in February, I was following my own rule. It was bedtime. I was staying awake as long as possible by playing The Frying Pan Game with my brother Orville.

To play The Frying Pan Game, you imagine that your bed is a giant frying pan. You act like food frying in the pan, and your brother has to guess what kind of food you are.

It was my turn. I stretched myself out on my bed and lay very still. Then I flipped over onto my stomach.

"A dead shark?" Orville whispered.

"NO!"

I flipped again.

"Pigs' feet?"

"NO!"

"Naked mole-rat brains?"

"I'm a pancake, Orville! What's wrong with you? I looked exactly like one!"

Orville grinned. "I thought you looked exactly like fried pigs' feet."

"Ha. Ha. Your turn."

Orville oozed onto his bed, wiggling his arms and legs.

"Noodles?"

"Nope."

"Green beans?"

"Nope."

"I give up."

Orville oozed some more. "I'm snot!" He started cracking up. "Who wants fried snot?" He wiggled over to my bed.

"Yuck! Go slime yourself!"

Mom appeared in the doorway. "Enough with the sliming. Go to sleep."

"How can we *go* to sleep if we don't know where it is?" I argued.

Orville giggled.

"Very funny," Mom said. "It's time to fall asleep."

"Fall asleep? Do Orville and I really *fall* when we sleep?"

"Good night!" Orville rolled out of bed and landed on the floor with a thud. I started cracking up.

"Get back in bed, Orville. Close your eyes, Wilbur."

"But how can I close my *eyes*? Eyes don't really close—"

"Close your eye*lids,* Wilbur! And no more laughing, Orville."

"Okay, no more laughing!" Orville threw himself onto his bed, closed his eyelids, and sang loudly: "On top of Old Smokey, all covered with snot, I dropped my poor mother. She screamed a whole lot!"

We both howled.

"You two are incorrigible."

"What does that mean?" I asked.

"I think it's a kind of cardboard," Orville said.

Mom laughed and turned out the light. "Good night!"

She stood outside the door, so we had to be quiet. I stared at the ceiling and practiced flaring my nostrils.

Flaring your nostrils is on The Riot Brother Top Ten List of Important Things to Be Able to Do with Your Face. You will find the complete list in *The Official Riot Brother Handbook* that I plan to publish in the near future.

Why, you ask, is being able to flare your nostrils so important?

Don't ask. It just is.

Anyway, I must have worn myself out practicing. As I heard my mom walking down the stairs, I felt myself falling asleep.

"Oh no!" I thought to myself. "I don't want to be falling asleep!"

A moment passed.

Then, this strange feeling came over me—or rather it came under me. My bed turned into a giant frying pan, and my room turned into the sea. "Either I'm in a giant frying pan floating on the sea," I thought to myself, "or else I'm dreaming."

Above me, the face of a huge naked mole-rat wearing a chef hat appeared. He grinned and flipped me with a monster-sized spatula. Up I flew, sailing toward the clouds. *Whee! I'm a bird! I'm a plane! Oh! No whee! I'm falling!*

I splashed into the sea and plunged down. A hundred sharks were swimming toward

me, their nostrils flaring. *Wait a minute! Do sharks have nostrils?* I looked around. *Where is an undersea library when you need one?* Yuck—the sharks' nostrils were filled with snot! They were coming closer—

A snorgling noise filled the room.

I sat up in my bed, thinking that I had been sprayed with shark snot. Then I realized I was safe in my bed.

The noise came again. Maybe I wasn't safe. The noise was real!

I listened. The snorgling came every few seconds.

It was clearly the sound of wild pig feet clawing through the wall by Orville's bed.

I turned on the bedside lamp. "Wake up, Orville," I whispered. "Wild pig attack!"

"What?" Orville sat up, and the snorgling stopped.

"Either a wild pig was busting the wall or else you were snoring."

Orville looked at the wall. "It was probably me. I'll try to wait until you fall asleep before I snore again, Wilbur."

"Thank you, Orville. For a third grader, you can be very thoughtful. Tomorrow, you may pick our mission."

"You're kidding?" His eyes got huge.

"As long as you don't pick capturing a bank robber or finding a hidden treasure because we've already done those."

"Right!" Orville said. "I'll think up a good one!"

"Excellent!" I said and turned off the light.

TWO
Snow Business

"I've got one." Orville jumped out of bed and turned on the light.

In case you were wondering: exactly one minute had passed since I had turned off the light.

"Let's overthrow a king!" he said.

I nodded. "Not too shabby, Orville. But it has to be a bad king. People don't overthrow good kings."

"Right!"

"And we both get to share the throne!"

"We can be king brothers!"

"There's only one tiny problem, Orville."

"What's that, Wilbur?"

"Tomorrow is a school day. It may be diffi-cult to overthrow a king and go to school at the same time."

Orville nodded. "We need a Snow Day."

I jumped out of bed. "Let's do The Secret Snow Day Ceremony."

"Bingo bongo!" Orville said.

What is The Secret Snow Day Ceremony, you ask?

I'll tell you. But don't tell anybody else. You do The Secret Snow Day Ceremony at night when you want to make it snow. Here's how:

1. Put your pajamas on backward.
2. Put white socks on your hands.
3. Wave your socky hands up high and chant: "Snow, Snow, do not stop. Pretty please with whipped cream on top!"

4. Throw your pillow in the air like a giant snowball and try to catch it with your head three times.
5. Go to sleep upside down.

We did all these things. After a few minutes of lying upside down in the darkness, Orville whispered: "Are you still awake?"

"Yes." I tried to scratch an itch on my nose with my sock.

"Wilbur, did this work the last time we tried it?"

"I don't remember," I said.

"Maybe we should do something more."

An idea leaped into my brain so fast it almost missed. "Let's make the ground outside white and when Mom opens the shades, she'll think it snowed."

Orville grinned. "And since she's the principal, she'll call off school."

How would we do it? We came up with some excellent possibilities.

WAYS TO MAKE FAKE SNOW

1. Pop a whole lot of popcorn and dump it on the ground and bushes.
2. Sprinkle flour all over the ground and bushes.
3. Spread white sheets on the ground and bushes.

Unfortunately, we could foresee a few tiny problems.

TINY PROBLEMS

1. What if owls, bats, raccoons, and possums eat all the popcorn before morning?
2. What if the flour mixes with dew and turns to papier-mâché?

3. What if clowns steal the sheets to
   make a new circus tent?

Tiny problems can lead to even bigger
problems.

EVEN BIGGER PROBLEMS
1. What if the owls, bats, raccoons,
   and possums eat too much, and
   their stomachs burst, and we
   have to clean up the yard?
2. What if the mailman comes just as
   the sun begins to shine, and the
   papier-mâché dries, and his feet get
   permanently stuck on our lawn?
3. What if the clowns later feel so
   guilty about stealing the sheets that
   they stop clowning around and the
   circus goes out of business?

Even bigger problems can lead to GIGAN-
TIC problems.

"We need a new plan," I said.

"How about we sneak around and tape white paper on all the windows?" Orville suggested. "In the morning, when Mom opens the shades she'll see white and think it snowed."

To tell you the truth, I knew it wasn't going to work. But the sneaking part sounded fun.

"Let's get to work!" I said.

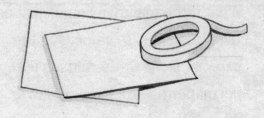

THREE
You Won't Believe This

When we ran downstairs in the morning, the shades were still down everywhere, except in the dining room where our mom was reading the newspaper. That shade was up, and the white paper we had taped on the window was there.

Last night, in the dark, the white paper looked like a blanket of snow. Now, the white paper looked like white paper. It couldn't have possibly fooled her.

Mom looked up from her newspaper. "Good morning, boys! Guess what?"

"It snowed?" Orville asked hopefully.

"Yes!"

Our mouths dropped open. The paper trick worked!

"School is officially canceled!"

Orville looked at me. I looked at Orville.

I gave him a Don't-Give-Our-Secret-Away look. But my insides were dancing and shouting: *We tricked her! We tricked her!*

Calmly, I turned to Mom. "What a surprise!"

"I know you want to play in the snow," she said. "But you have to eat breakfast first."

"Oh, we don't want to play in the snow," I said.

Orville looked surprised. "I do!"

"No, you don't," I whispered. "We have to overthrow a king, remember?"

"But I'd rather play in the snow."

I pulled Orville into the bathroom and lifted up the shade. "Orville, there isn't any snow! We tricked her."

Orville looked at the white paper taped on the window. "I forgot."

We walked back into the dining room.

"We don't want to play in the snow," Orville said.

Mom stared at us. "Something strange happened last night, didn't it?"

We froze. Did she know about the paper?

She leaned forward and looked at us

suspiciously. "You're aliens from Mars. And you've kidnapped my real children! The real Wilbur and Orville wouldn't want to stay inside on a Snow Day."

Orville and I looked at each other with relief. "Ha! Ha! Ha!" We laughed.

"Now I know you're aliens! My boys never laugh at my jokes."

"Ha! Ha! Ha!" We laughed even louder.

"Wilbur," Orville whispered after we stopped laughing. "What exactly does it mean to overthrow a king?"

"It was your idea."

"I know. But just because it was my idea doesn't mean I understand it."

"It means to kick the bad king out and take his place as a good king."

"But how do we do the overthrowing? Do we need some kind of overthrowing machine?"

For a minute, I was stumped. I hadn't thought about how we were going to actually do the overthrowing. A machine sounded handy. "I've got it!" I said. "Let's invent a catapult with a chair attached to it. We'll give it to the king and say: 'Here is your new throne, Your Majesty.' And when the king sits in the chair . . . *Whoosh!!* He'll go flying! We'll call it The King Flinger."

"Or we can put mashed potatoes in the chair and fling them into his face!" Orville grinned. "We can call it The Thing to Fling Things at the King with a Zing!"

"Not too shabby," I said. "How about The Flinger for short?"

FOUR
Flinging

Unfortunately, you weren't in our basement to see the actual making of The Flinger. But you can see our official sketches. We modeled it after the teeter-totter. The idea was that when one of us jumped on the end, the king would fly off the throne.

After we finished, we wanted to test it. "I get to be the king," Orville said.

"I should be the king," I argued. "I'm older."

"I'm lighter. I'll fly better."

I hate it when Orville is right.

I pretended to take off a pretend hat. "Your Majesty, may it pleaseth you. We have brought you a new throne."

Orville frowned. "You dirtbag! Why would I wanteth a new throne? My old throne is fine!"

"Your Majesty, you needeth a new throne because you have such a . . . kingly bottom. Your royal rear is worth a thousand dirtbags!"

"You're right, O Lowly Servant. I have the finest bottom in all the land." Orville stuck out his rear and sang: "O everyone loves my fine, fine bottom!" He hopped into the chair, and I climbed up onto the washing machine.

"Your Majesty. I bid you farewell . . ." I jumped onto the end of The Flinger.

Orville went flying . . . into me!

"Wwwhhhooooaa!" We screamed and landed with a crash in a pile of empty boxes.

I pulled a box off my head.

Riot Brother Rule #8: When you see something flinging toward your head, duck.

"Ouch," Orville said. He pulled his leg out of the mess and shook his foot, which was jammed into an empty Doodie Diaper Wipe container. Our mom is very crafty. She collects empty diaper wipe boxes to store craft supplies. "I think my foot is stuck forever."

Mom walked in. "Don't tell me. You're inventing again. What is it?"

Orville looked at me. I could tell what he was thinking. We love it when our mom says:

"Don't tell me," because then we can keep our secrets.

"Wait, let me guess!" Mom said. "You're inventing a mess?"

"Ha, ha, ha," I laughed.

Orville stuck a Doodie Diaper Wipe box on his other foot and stood up. "We're inventing new boots!" He shuffled around with the boxes on his feet. "Doodie boots!"

"Yes!" I said. "See how the plastic containers will protect shoes from the snow!"

I squashed my feet into Doodie Diaper Wipe boxes. "And they're so comfortable!"

"And Doodie cheap!" Orville said. He slid around the basement floor.

I held out my arms. "You've heard of snowboards. Well these are snow boots. You can slide around on the snow with them."

Orville did a running slide, falling down at the end. "They're great for wiping out!"

"We call them Wipe-Out Boots," I exclaimed.

"Doodie Wipe-Out Boots!"

"Doodie Dude Wipe-Out Boots!"

Mom laughed. "And what's this?" She looked at The Flinger.

"That is a machine for . . . uh . . ."

"Wait! Let me guess. It's a machine for throwing snowballs!" she said.

Orville looked at me. I looked at Orville. "Not too shabby!" we said.

Mom laughed. "Hey! I finally guessed right!"

Riot Brother Rule #9:
Every once in a while,
let grown-ups think they're right.

"Speaking of snow," she said. "Why don't you test it outside?"

Orville and I froze.

"You can try your new boots, too, but only if you promise to be careful."

Mom picked up one side of The Flinger. "I'll help you carry it out!"

"No!" I jumped in to take her place. "We can do it by ourselves, right, Orville?"

Orville looked at me as if I was crazy. "But Wilbur, don't you remember?" He mouthed the words: "No snow?"

I made one of my famous Just-Go-Along-With-It faces. "We'd love to play in the snow *all by ourselves,* wouldn't we, Orville?"

Orville nodded, getting it. If Mom went out and discovered there was no snow, we'd be in big trouble. "You stay inside and keep warm, Mom."

Quickly we carried The Flinger up the stairs. This is not an easy thing to do when you're wearing diaper-wipe containers on your feet.

"Wait!" I cried. I felt a saying coming on.

Orville balanced on the middle step and listened politely.

I cleared my throat. "Do not judge a person," I said, "until you have walked in his diaper-wipe boxes for two moons."

"I don't get it," Orville said.

"Wait! I feel another saying coming on." I cleared my throat. "If you say something and nobody gets it, say something else."

"Will you stop saying sayings, Wilbur!"

"Okay. How about this?" I cleared my throat and made the loudest burp ever.

Orville laughed.

"If you say something and nobody gets it, burp."

Orville nodded. "Now that's a good one."

FIVE
Down with the King

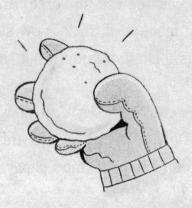

We put on our hats, coats, and mittens and carried our machine out the door. I was walking backward, holding onto the chair part.

The light was blinding.

Squinting, we set down The Flinger in the snow and—

Orville looked at me. I looked at Orville. His eyes were huge. "It snowed!" we both screamed.

Our street is the best street for sledding because it's very steep. And our house is the best house because it's at the top of the street on a hill of its own. From our front yard, we can see the universe. And today, a glittering blanket of thick snow sparkled all around us. "Do you know what this means, Orville?"

"Our Secret Snow Day Ceremony worked?"

"Yes! Do you know what else this means?"

"We didn't have to tape paper on all the windows?"

"Yes. Do you know what else this means?"

"We could have been playing in the snow all morning?"

"Yes. Do you know what else—"

I didn't get to finish my sentence because . . .

BAM! Something hard hit me right on the back.

A familiar voice bellowed. "WHO AM I?"

Goliath Hyke, the boss of the neighborhood, stood in the street. All the other kids were out, too. Even Tiffany, Jonathan Kemp's two-year-old sister, was toddling around in her pink snowsuit. Orville and I were the only ones who had been inside.

"WHO AM I?" Goliath bellowed again.

"The Snowball King," everybody mumbled. It sounded as if he had already made them say it fifty times.

He grabbed a snowball from his sled, which was piled with snowballs. He threw it at a bird perched on the telephone pole.

BAM! The bird squawked and flew away.

"WHO AM I?"

"The Snowball King."

He grabbed an armful and pitched them at Doom, the beastly brown dog fenced in on the corner. Doom howled and threw himself at the fence. Goliath laughed, grabbed another, and threw it at Tiffany. BAM! She fell into a snowbank and disappeared. All you could see were her shining pink boots.

"Hey!" Jonathan yelled.

"Hey what?" Goliath sneered.

"Nothing." Jonathan helped his sister out of the snowbank.

"Hey Kemp?" Goliath yelled.

Jonathan looked up.

Goliath got him right in the face with a snowball. "Sorry, I forgot to tell you to duck!" He laughed. "The Snowball King rules supreme!"

My blood started to boil. "Come on, Orville! Let's put snowballs on this thing and see if it can fling."

I stepped toward a big pile of snow, forgetting about my Doodie Dude Wipe-Out Boots. "Whoa!" I slid and landed on my rear.

Goliath laughed. "Check out the Riot Brothers! Their mom makes them wear Doodie Wipes!"

"Our mom didn't make us do anything!" Orville shouted. "We invented them."

Goliath laughed harder.

We piled snowballs in the throne.

"You're history!" I called out.

I stood on the top doorstep and jumped onto the end of The Flinger. This time I ducked.

Snowballs flew.

It is a beautiful thing when snowballs seem to *want* to land on Goliath Hyke's head. They knocked off his pointy hat.

Everybody clapped.

Now *his* blood was boiling. "I'm using that machine!" He came running and sliding up our steep driveway.

"No way!" Orville started to say, but I elbowed him.

"Sure, Goliath!" I said. "But it's not really for throwing snowballs."

Goliath looked at me suspiciously. "What's it for?"

"It's a throne," I whispered.

Orville grinned at me. "For a king!" he added.

I gestured to the chair. "If you sit in the throne, we'll raise you up. From that height, you can really throw snowballs far."

Goliath tugged on his hat. "Why would you help me?"

I looked at Orville. Why would we help Goliath Hyke?

"We *have* to help you," Orville said quickly. "You're the King."

Goliath couldn't argue with that. He grinned, grabbed a few snowballs, and hopped into the chair.

"Royal feet need royal boots, Your Majesty!" Orville said and shoved his diaper wipe boxes on Goliath's feet.

The kids in the street were nervous. "Hey, what's going on?" Margaret called.

"This is my throne!" Goliath yelled happily. "They're going to raise me up."

Orville and I both stood on the top step.

The kids couldn't believe what was happening. The Riot Brothers were actually helping Goliath Hyke?

"We'll have to both jump hard," I whispered to Orville. "Don't forget to duck."

"Your Majesty, fareweeeeellllllll!" We linked arms and jumped.

"Wwwwwhhhooooooooaaaaa!" Goliath flew over our heads like a wild pig flipped out of a frying pan. He landed on his Wipe-Out Boots and sailed down our hill into the street. The kids screamed and scattered. "Help!" he yelled as he slid through the crowd and began to slide down the steep road. "I can't stop!" He was waving his arms like crazy and yelling his brains out. Orville and I scampered down our hill and stood with the others in the street. We watched him go and go and go and go until he was just a tiny bit of scrapple in the distance.

I felt a pull on my jacket and there was Tiffany Kemp, staring up at me with red cheeks and a runny nose. "Goyiath go bye bye?" she asked.

"Yes," I said and waved at the disappearing speck. "Bye bye, Goyiath!"

"Where he go?" Tiffany asked.

"All the way to Mexico!" Orville said.

Everybody laughed and crowded around us.

"That was great!"

"You guys are awesome!"

"Those boots are cool!"

Jonathan Kemp's voice raised above the others. "The Riot Brothers are the real Snowball Kings!"

"Did you hear that, Orville? We did it! We overthrew a king!"

"And now we're the new king brothers!"

I turned to face our adoring crowd. "We promise to be good kings!"

Orville grinned. "We will give everyone free candy!"

Everybody cheered.

I pulled off Orville's hat. "Are you crazy? We can't afford to give everybody free candy."

"What can we afford to do?"

A thought came to me like a snowball out of the blue. "We can give everybody free Doodie Dude Wipe-Out Boots!"

Orville and I ran downstairs and got all the diaper wipe boxes we could find. While the kids squashed their feet into them, we loaded the throne with snowballs and sent them flying through the air like fireworks.

A van turned the corner and stopped at our house. The driver unrolled his window. "Cool machine!" he said. Across the side of his van *The Daily News* was written.

"We invented it!" Orville said. "And the boots, too!"

"I'd like to take a photo of you for the newspaper. Can you ask your mom or dad if it's all right?"

Mom came out and signed the release form.

"Will we be in the newspaper tomorrow?" Orville asked.

The man pulled a large camera out of his black bag. "Depends on how the pictures turn out."

"We're going to be famous!" Orville grinned as we stood on either side of the machine.

"That's great! Just hold it!" The photographer positioned himself.

"Flare your nostrils," I whispered to Orville.

We flared. The photographer snapped.

"The Snowball Kings!" shouted the kids. And we all started running around throwing snowballs at each other like maniacs.

Let me tell you, it is a beautiful thing to see a bunch of kids slip-sliding around on a Snow Day with diaper wipe boxes on their feet.

SIX

Hear Ye! Hear Ye!

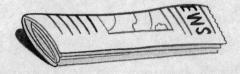

The next morning, Orville poked me awake. We ran downstairs.

Mom was already up, reading the paper.

"Are we in it?" we both asked.

"Sorry, boys," she said. "You're not in the paper...YOU'RE ON THE FRONT PAGE!" She smiled and held up the newspaper. There we were with nostrils flaring!

The Snowball Kings

Delighted by the unexpected snowfall yesterday, Orville (left) and Wilbur (right) Riot invented a snowball-throwing machine called The Flinger.

Although there was still lots of snow on the ground, the streets were clear, so we had to go to school. But that was okay because we were famous! Jonathan Kemp taped copies of the newspaper on our lockers. Everybody wanted our autographs.

Except Goliath Hyke, of course.

At lunch, Jonathan and Orville ran over to my table in the cafeteria. "You gotta see something." Jonathan glanced nervously in the direction of Goliath.

They pulled me down the hall to my locker. Somebody had drawn mustaches on the picture of Orville and me.

"What do you bet it was Goliath!" Jonathan said. "What are you going to do about it?"

"We can't let Goliath get away with this," I said.

Orville looked closer at the photo. "Hey, I think I look cool with a mustache!"

"I've got it!" I said. I opened my locker and pulled out a black marker. "Give me your face, Orville!"

I drew mustaches fit for a king on my brother and on me.

We walked back into the cafeteria with our mustaches. "Flare your nostrils," I whispered.

Everybody went crazy, laughing and clapping.

Orville bowed.

"Wait!" I said. A saying was coming to me.

Orville listened politely.

"It is better to make a fool out of yourself," I whispered, "than to allow someone else to make a fool out of you."

"Good one, O King Wilbur."

"Thank you, King Mustachio!"

That night, Mom said we had had such an exciting day, we should go to bed early. Grown-ups don't have a clue. If you have had an exciting day, you want to stay up especially late to make it last as long as possible. But you know that.

Anyway, a few minutes after Mom made us turn off the lights, Orville and I heard the sound of music coming from the living room downstairs.

We like it whenever our mom decides to play her cello at night, because whenever she plays her cello at night she seems to forget about checking up on us.

I turned on the lights.

"Okay, I got a good one," Orville said. "Guess what I am." He rolled himself into a ball and made a sizzling sound.

"A meatball?"

"No."

"A potato?"

"Wrong-o."

"An onion!"

"Nope. I'm a fried snowball."

"You can't fry a snowball."

"Why not?"

"It would melt."

"Well, what you've got when it melts is called Fried Snowball."

"What you've got when it melts is called water."

"Maybe not. Maybe there's something in snowflakes that makes the water crusty if you cook it. Let's get a snowball and try it right now!"

For an onion-head, Orville sometimes has fun ideas.

We snuck out of bed and tiptoed downstairs. Quietly, we slipped our bare feet into our regular boots, grabbed our mittens, and crept out the back door without our coats.

The night was black and cold and silent, except for the crunching of our boots on the snow and the singing of the cello behind us, which sounded very far away. We walked to the middle of our backyard and stopped. Yesterday, and after school today, we had played in the front, so the snow back here was untouched.

Orville made a kind of gasp in his throat. "This is the best kind of snow," he whispered. "The no-footprint kind."

I nodded, and we looked at the world stretched out, glistening in the moonlight.

Then Orville took a breath. "I feel like it's all here . . . just for us."

"For the Riot Brothers." I plunged my boot into fresh snow. "For the Riot Brother Kings!"

"Look, Wilbur."

Tiny new snowflakes were falling out of

the black night. It was as if the sky were shaking loose its stars for us.

We held out our mittens to catch them.

"Hey Wilbur, what if we could have as many adventures as there are snowflakes falling right now?"

"I would be disappointed in us if we didn't try, Orville."

We scooped up handfuls of snow. Perfect snowball snow.

"Before we go inside and try our Fried Snowball experiment," I suggested, "perhaps we should see what other uses we can find for these?" I held up two snowballs and flared my nostrils.

"Bingo bongo," Orville cried.

What happened then, you ask?

Let's just say that Orville does some fine, fine dancing when he has snow down his pants!

The End

P. S. Riot Brother Rule #10: If you draw a mustache on your face, make sure you don't use permanent ink.

BONUS!

You have just finished reading three Riot Brother books rolled into one. In this bonus section, you will find the Riot Brother Games, Rules, and Sayings mentioned in this book all laid out for you like food on a picnic table. Whenever you're hungry for a little Riot Brother fun or wisdom, you'll know right where to turn. And as an extra, free bonus, I'm throwing in The Top Ten List of Important Things to Be Able to Do with Your Face.

You are really going to get your money's worth out of this book. Of course, if you checked this book out of the library, then you are really, really going to get your money's worth because you didn't spend any money on it.

RIOT BROTHER GAMES

You can play these games with brothers, or sisters, or friends, if you've got them. Just don't try to play with a grown-up who won't laugh at a decent joke even if it comes flying out of his or her nose.

Snarf Attack

The object of the game is to make your opponent snarf. Before dinner starts, agree to play the game. During dinner, try to say or do something that will make your opponent laugh really hard while he or she is drinking milk. If the milk comes out his or her mouth, that's just called dribbling and doesn't count. If the milk comes out his or her nose, that's a genuine snarf, and you win. Whoever loses has to slurp up the snarfed milk (just kidding—ha ha!).

Underfoodle

(Note: if you are playing this game with friends instead of your brother or sister, it is polite to use clean underwear.) The object of the game is to see who can get the most underwear on his or her head in exactly thirty seconds. This is a complex game, which requires skill and strategy. Not only must you put underpants on your own head and guard them against attack, but also you must try to pull underpants off your opponent's head. The loser has to wear underpants on his or her head to school the next day (just kidding—ha ha ha!).

The Naked Mole-Rat Game

You and your opponent each get a cracker, a piece of toast, or something crunchy. Pick any number higher than three. This number is called the Bite Target. The object of the game is to reach the Bite Target by eating the crunchy thing in the exact number of bites as the Bite Target.

Why can't you pick a number lower than three, you ask? There are two reasons. 1) The more bites you have to take, the funnier it is. 2) If you tried to eat a whole piece of toast in only one or two bites, you might choke and then barf up the pieces. (Orville used to do this all the time.) You automatically lose the game if you choke and barf. Loser has to clean up the barf (*not* kidding—ha ha!).

The Frying Pan Game

The object of the game is to do such a fine job of acting like some kind of fried food that your fellow player will guess what kind of food you are. To play, imagine that your bed is a giant frying pan. Get in and make it look like you are the food. Remember that food sizzles and flops around a lot in a hot pan, so use your whole body. You may also use your voice for sound effects. This is an excellent game to play while on vacation because hotel beds are so big and bouncy. But do *not* play this game in a tent, especially if your tent is small and the stakes have not been firmly hammered into the ground, because the tent will collapse (not kidding) and a grown-up will make you eat fried snot for breakfast (just kidding—ha ha ha ha ha!).

RIOT BROTHER RULES

1. Make something exciting happen every day.
2. Do not tell anyone your true mission.
3. If someone says, "Don't look now!" make sure you look.
4. Run, do not walk, whenever possible.
5. Don't change your mission in the middle of the day.
6. Talk softly even if you think you're alone, because grown-ups have excellent hearing.

7. Stay awake as long as possible.
8. When you see something flinging toward your head, duck.
9. Every once in a while, let grown-ups think they're right.
10. If you draw a mustache on your face, make sure you don't use permanent ink.

RIOT BROTHER SAYINGS

—All you need is a butt to put underpants on your butt, but it takes a brain to put underpants on your head.

—Life is like the mail. You can't count on something exciting to come through the slot.

—There is nothing quite as frightening as your mom chasing after you with kissy lips.

—Do not judge a person, until you have walked in his diaper wipe boxes for two moons.

—If you say something and nobody gets it, say something else.

—If you say something and nobody gets it, burp.

—It is better to make a fool out of yourself than to allow someone else to make a fool out of you.

THE RIOT BROTHER TOP TEN LIST OF IMPORTANT THINGS TO BE ABLE TO DO WITH YOUR FACE

Face it. Your face is the most important part of your body. People stare at your face all the time. Who stares at your kneecaps?

You can say stuff with your face without using words. How cool. Learning how to do things with your face will also keep you from being bored. Even if you have to sit quietly in school, you can entertain yourself by practicing clever facial stunts. If your face is facing a friend, then you will also keep your friend from being bored. How very nice of you and your face!

So, here's what you should learn to do.

1. **Raise one eyebrow.**
   If someone asks you a stupid question, this is an excellent response.

2. **Make your eyebrows jump up and down.**
   Think of your eyebrows as little pets that live on your face.

3. **Flare your nostrils.**
   Bullfighters do this. They got the idea from bulls.

4. **Pinch your nostrils closed, then snort upward.**
   This makes your nose look like it got squished between elevator doors.

5. **Wiggle your ears.**
   Do this, and you won't look human.

6. **Do tongue tricks: roll it, fold it, twist it, curl it, touch it to your nose.**
   If you have a school talent show, your tongue could be the star.

7. **Hold a pencil between your nose and upper lip.**

Don't use your hands. Now, wiggle your mouth to make the pencil go crazy. Do the same thing with your chin on your desk. Voila! Your face has become a drummer.

8. **Look without looking as if you are looking.**

Very handy if you are a spy or a crook catcher.

9. **Look like you have no idea what just happened.**

Very handy if you have just done something wrong and a grown-up is staring at you.

10. **Look like you're going to throw up.**

Very handy if you don't like what's for dinner.

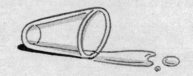